ABOVE ALL:

Be In Health (3 John 1:2)

Dr. Dean Melton

Edited and Compiled By Roberta K. Dawson
With Foreword by Andrew Wommack

Copyright © 2009 by Pastor Dean Melton

Above All: Be In Health (3 John 1:2)

All rights reserved. No part of this book may be reproduced or transmitted in any form or by any means, electronic, or mechanical, including photocopying, recording or by any information storage and retrieval system, without permission in writing from the publisher. No abridgement or changes to the text are authorized by the publisher.

All scripture references are from the King James version of the Holy Bible unless otherwise notated

ISBN number: 978-1-59712-376-1

Printed in the United States of America by
Catawba Publishing Company

Order from:
Catawba Publishing Company
(704) 717-8452
www.catawbapublishing.com

Contents

Who Are You Listening To?	1
Lazarus, Come Forth!	7
Healed at the Pool	13
An Eye Made of Mud	19
Pigs and Demons	25
Jesus Stops The Bleeding	33
A Dead Girl Lives	39
A Brand New Set of Legs	43
Abiding in the Vine	49
Healing is for Today	53
Your Time Is Now	67

Foreword

Many people believe God can heal and they occasionally receive a healing much like a blind squirrel still finds a nut every once in awhile. But few people believe God has already done His part, has given us His power to heal, and also the authority to exercise that power. That is a totally different approach. Pastor Dean Melton is one of those who knows it is God's will to heal and has put his faith into action with miraculous results.

I've known Pastor Dean since 1987 when I first spoke at his Campmeeting. I've been a regular at Freedom Christian Center's Campmeeting now for over 22 years and the Lord has mightily impacted my life through this man of God. Some of the most significant things the Lord has spoken to me have come through Pastor Dean Melton.

Pastor Dean has seen multiple people raised from the dead. I've seen him personally deal with and overcome a bout with Shingles through using his faith. He stood strong when the doctors told him there was no hope for his wife, Georgia, and today she's still with us.

In this book you will truly come to believe that God

wants you to be in health and prosper. You will not only read testimonies of God's miraculous healing power but you will gain insight into how a man of faith gets these supernatural results. It will inspire you and challenge you to believe God for more and we all need that.

   Andrew Wommack
   Andrew Wommack Ministries
   Colorado, USA

Foreword

My name is Darey Jolley and my wife Karen and I have served as Associate Pastors for nearly twenty-five years under the leadership of Dr. Dean Melton, my father in the Lord.

I would like to tell you that over these years I have personally seen and experienced the miracles you will read about in this book. I have come to trust and believe in the anointing that God has place on Dr. Melton's life.

Dr. Melton has faithfully served his people with all of his heart. I believe in these last days, God is looking for the church to begin to flow in the miraculous – not only in word, but also in action. I am convinced without a doubt that Dr. Melton is doing just that.

We have seen these mighty works not only in the United States of America, but also in the nations of the world. For the last 20 years, Dr. Melton has carried this healing message to various countries. He established an outreach called Ambassadors To The Nations. Today, Ambassadors To The Nations reaches many countries including Cuba, Mexico, Jamaica, and Nicaragua.

I hope you will take time to enjoy this book. I know it

will be a blessing to you.

In His Service,
Darey Jolley

Who Are You Listening To?

Beloved, I wish above all things that thou mayest prosper and be in health, even as thy soul prospereth (3 John 1:2 KJV).

Let me start off by saying this is not another book about prosperity. Now don't get me wrong. I believe in prosperity. I believe that God wants us to prosper. He doesn't care if we have truckloads of money, two or three houses and a different car to drive every day of the week. But what I want to focus on is the healing part. That's why I've turned the scripture around. Above all, I want you to be in health and prosper. Folks, if you are healthy, you can get a million dollars. But if you are sick, all the money in the world can't buy your healing. What would you rather have: your health or millions of dollars that you can't even enjoy?

If you are reading this book, either you need healing or you know someone who needs healing. This book is intended to show you, by the scriptures, God's plan and purpose regarding the healing of our physical bodies.

The first thing to consider when you begin to study healing is who are you listening to? There are teachings everywhere. Some are of the opinion that God is not in the healing business today. Some believe that sometimes God heals, sometimes He doesn't. Others, like me, believe that it is God's will to heal every single person every single time. I believe that God wants us healed so that we can accomplish the work that he has for us to do here on this Earth. That's what I teach the people at my church.

The people that you listen to feed your spirit. This is true about healing as well as every other subject that you have been taught about. If you hear something often enough, you will eventually start to believe it. Let's look at two men in the bible. The first one is Diotrophes. Here is 3 John 1:9-12(NLT) John was writing to his friend Gaius.

9 I wrote to the church about this, but Diotrephes, who loves to be the leader, refuses to have anything to do with us. 10 When I come, I will report some of the things he is doing and the evil accusations he is making against us. Not only does he refuse to welcome the traveling teachers, he also tells others not to help them. And when they do help, he puts them out of the church.

Diotrephes is symbolic of some people today. People use their position and charisma to persuade others to view healing in a certain way. Let's say that "preacher A" does not believe in healing. He does not believe that God ever heals anyone. He may even believe that God uses sickness and disease to teach us a lesson. The beliefs of this "preacher" will eventually become the beliefs of those that follow him. The people who sit in his

Above All: Be In Health (3 John 1:2)

congregation will begin to believe that they deserve to be sick. They deserve to have cancer. They may think that they are just "suffering for Jesus." All this is based on what the "preacher" teaches and believes.

In verse 10, John continues to write that not only does Diotrephes refuse to hear the truths of God, but he also forbids others from listening to and welcoming the truth. This is a dangerous situation. Diotrephes even went so far as to kick people out of his church if they dared to believe or follow anything other than what he taught. Don't let the Diotrephes spirit rule you. Be strong enough to study out God's word relating to healing and then make up your mind for yourself. Look at 3 John 1 again.

In verse 11, writes: Dear friend, don't let this bad example influence you. Follow only what is good. Remember that those who do good prove that they are God's children, and those who do evil prove that they do not know God. (NLT)

John was telling Gaius not to let people like Diotrephes influence him. Don't let people who don't believe in healing influence you. The second part of the verse says it very plainly. People who don't believe in healing do not know God. That is not to say that they aren't saved or that they can't go to heaven. It simply means that they don't really know what God has said about healing. In verse 12, John talks about a good man of God named Demetrius.

12 Everyone says good things about Demetrius, and the truth agrees with what they say. We also speak well of him, and you know what we say is true. (New Century Version)

In contrast to Diotrephes, Demetrius was a godly man. Everyone spoke highly of him. I believe that in order to receive your healing, you must listen to and learn from those who know the truths of God concerning healing. Surround yourself with people who believe that you can be healed. There is no room for doubt. Everyone you come into contact with should know what you believe about healing. If they don't believe like you – if they have the Diotrephes spirit – then you can't afford to hang around them. Any little bit of doubt can cause you to falter and miss your healing.

Don't listen to people who teach that God is not in the healing business today. I came to tell you that it is the will of God to heal everyone who is sick. If you are not walking in total and complete healing, then you have to make up your mind. If you decide that God is your healer, then don't listen to anyone who tells you otherwise.

Jesus is a healer. Acts 10:36-39 reads like this:

36 The word which God sent unto the children of Israel, preaching peace by Jesus Christ: (he is Lord of all:)37 That word, I say, ye know, which was published throughout all Judaea, and began from Galilee, after the baptism which John preached; 38 How God anointed Jesus of Nazareth with the Holy Ghost and with power: who went about doing good, and healing all that were oppressed of the devil; for God was with him.39And we are witnesses of all things which he did both in the land of the Jews, and in Jerusalem; whom they slew and hanged on a tree: (KJV)

Look at verse 38. How God anointed Jesus. According to the Jewish tradition, whenever someone was anointed with the specific Holy anointing oil formula and ceremony described in Exodus 30:22-25, the Spirit of God came upon this person, to qualify him or her for a God-given task. Jesus did not go through this type of anointing ceremony. Rather, God Himself anointed Jesus. God gave His power to Jesus. Jesus was able to operate in healing because He was anointed with the Holy Spirit of God.

Jesus went about doing good. He did not stay in one place and wait for people to come to him. Instead, he went to the people. He traveled from place to place and everywhere he went, he healed people. He went about doing good. Jesus did only good works. It doesn't say that Jesus went about putting sickness on people. No, he went about healing them. So Jesus is a healer. He is not the one who makes us sick. He makes us well. When we settle it in our mind that Jesus is a healer, we will never again blame Him for sickness and disease.

Many people cannot receive their healing because they cannot see Jesus as a healer. Because of the wrong teaching people receive, they believe that God puts us through things to make us stronger and better. Let me ask you a question. If you had a sick baby and you prayed that God would heal that baby, do you think that you would be stronger and a better Christian if your baby died? No! You would be stronger and better if you saw your baby totally healed by the power of Jesus Christ.

Don't believe that Jesus or God make you sick. That is not the truth. Jesus said it plainly in John 10:10.

The thief cometh not, but for to steal, and to kill, and to destroy: I am come that they might have life, and that they might have it more abundantly.

It is this simple: Jesus is the healer and the devil is the one who makes us sick. You have to settle that in your mind. Only then can you truly receive your healing.

Lazarus, Come Forth!

If you have been a Christian any length of time, I know you have read or heard the story of Lazarus. There are a lot of things about healing that we can learn from this man's story.

1Now a certain man was sick, named Lazarus, of Bethany, the town of Mary and her sister Martha. 2(It was that Mary which anointed the Lord with ointment, and wiped his feet with her hair, whose brother Lazarus was sick.) 3Therefore his sisters sent unto him, saying, Lord, behold, he whom thou lovest is sick. (John 11:1-3 KJV)

It said Lazarus was sick. It is important to understand that when this all started, Lazarus was not dead. He was sick. Mary and Martha tried to manipulate Jesus. They sent word to Jesus – " Jesus the one who you love is sick." They implied that Jesus loved Lazarus more than you or me. Has the devil ever lied to you and told you that you can't receive your healing because you're not good enough? You're not holy enough? God loves sister so and so more than He loves you? I came along to tell you that is not the truth. Jesus loves us all equally and wants us all to be healed.

Look at verse 4. Jesus said, "This sickness is not unto death." How we respond to a situation determines what outcome we will receive. Jesus said this sickness is not going to kill Lazarus. If the sisters had believed that, then we would be reading a very different story. The sisters and the people around them could not receive what Jesus said. Lets read on.

6When he had heard therefore that he was sick, he abode two days still in the same place where he was.

Jesus loved Lazarus and he loved Mary and Martha. Yet when he knew that Lazarus was sick, he stayed right where he was. Jesus did not get in a hurry. He refused to let people manipulate him. I'm telling you we have to be the same way. We have to know what God has said about healing and we have to be bold enough to stand on that Word and not move quickly.

Once there was a family in my church who called me to report that their son was dying. My wife and I were at the beach and they called me to tell me that their son's nervous system was shutting down and that the doctors had said that if there wasn't a miracle, the boy would die. Now that little boy was about four or five years old and his mother and father wanted their son to live. They said "Pastor you have to come right now." I knew that God was not saying for me to go right at that moment. So I stayed right where I was. I waited four days and then I started back towards Charlotte. I intended to go straight to the hospital, but on the way home, the Lord spoke to me and told me to follow my normal routine.

"What would you normally do?" He asked. "I would go home and unpack the car and then ride by the church", I responded.

Acting on the Lord's instructions, I did just that. I went home, unpacked the car and by the time I got to the hospital that night, it was about 9:00 pm. The little boy's family was distraught. "Pastor, if you'd only come, our son would have been okay", they said. I knew that God had told me to wait, so I was not moved by what they said. The doctors had said that the little boy would not live through the night. But, I believed the report of the Lord. I went to the little boy's bedside and prayed, in faith, that God would perform a miracle. I spoke to his nervous system and commanded him to live. By 11:00 that night, the little boy had started improving. The doctors could not understand what had happened, but they started taking the tubes out of the little boy's body. Folks, I'm telling you two days later, that little boy went home. He was totally healed by the power of God! Let me tell you again: a person of faith does not move in a hurry. If you do that, you may miss God.

When Jesus knew that it was time to go to Lazarus, he said to the disciples:

11…. our friend Lazarus sleepeth; but I go, that I may awake him out of sleep. 12Then said his disciples, Lord, if he sleep, he shall do well. 13Howbeit Jesus spake of his death: but they thought that he had spoken of taking of rest in sleep. 14Then said Jesus unto them plainly, Lazarus is dead. 15And I am glad for your sakes that I was not there, to the intent ye may believe; nevertheless let us go unto him (John 11:11-14)

Look at this. Jesus knew that Lazarus was dead. He

had to make it plain for the disciples. They just weren't getting it. They thought that Jesus was saying that Lazarus was sleeping. They said, " that's good – we all need to rest." Jesus finally had to tell them "Lazarus is dead." I mean can you get any plainer than that? But Jesus knew the plan of God. He knew that even though Lazarus was dead, God's glory was going to make him come alive again.

Verse 17 : Then when Jesus came, he found that he had lain in the grave four days already. It is significant that Lazarus had been dead for four days. According to ancient Jewish tradition, it is said that the soul remained near the body for three days but by the fourth day a person was truly considered to be dead. So Lazarus was not just dead. He was really dead by the time Jesus got there.

Look at verse 19: And many of the Jews came to Martha and Mary, to comfort them concerning their brother. Watch out when the "comforters" come. You have to be careful. People will say all sorts of things. "Well brother I know someone who had that and they died in four weeks." "Well sister maybe God is just trying to teach you a lesson." "You never can tell; maybe God just needed her more than we did." Folks that's ridiculous. When you are sick, get around people who are going to lift you up, not push you further down. Get around people who will tell you what God has already said about your healing. You need people who will speak the Word and speak the Word only. People told Mary and Martha so much junk that Martha couldn't receive it when Jesus said (verse 25) "I am the resurrection, and the life: he that believeth in me, though he were dead, yet shall he live: 26And whosoever liveth and believeth in me shall never die. Believest thou this?" Martha called Jesus Lord. But, because of all the negativity and doubt that people had been feeding her, she couldn't really believe that He was able to bring her brother back to life.

You know the story. Jesus went on to call Lazarus forth from the grave. 43And when he thus had spoken, he cried with a loud voice, Lazarus, come forth. By the sheer power of Jesus voice, Lazarus got up! Augustine, a fourth century theologian, said that it was good that Jesus called Lazarus by name or else the whole cemetery would have come out of the grave. I'm telling you folks we have that same power today. We can call forth our healing.

Verse 44 …And he that was dead came forth, bound hand and foot with graveclothes: and his face was bound about with a napkin. Jesus saith unto them, Loose him, and let him go.

The last point I want to make about this story is this. When we receive our healing, we have to do something in order to keep it. Notice that Jesus did the miracle and Lazarus came out of the grave. But when Lazarus came forth, Jesus commanded the people to do something. He told them to take Lazarus's grave clothes off. It is so important that you surround yourself with likeminded people. You need people who are going to remind you that you were healed, that you are healed. Don't let the "comforters" talk you out of your healing. Lazarus sure didn't!

Dr. Dean Melton

Healed at the Pool

1After this there was a feast of the Jews; and Jesus went up to Jerusalem. 2Now there is at Jerusalem by the sheep market a pool, which is called in the Hebrew tongue Bethesda, having five porches. 3In these lay a great multitude of impotent folk, of blind, halt, withered, waiting for the moving of the water. 4For an angel went down at a certain season into the pool, and troubled the water: whosoever then first after the troubling of the water stepped in was made whole of whatsoever disease he had. 5And a certain man was there, which had an infirmity thirty and eight years. 6When Jesus saw him lie, and knew that he had been now a long time in that case, he saith unto him, Wilt thou be made whole? 7The impotent man answered him, Sir, I have no man, when the water is troubled, to put me into the pool: but while I am coming, another steppeth down before me. 8Jesus saith unto him, Rise, take up thy bed, and walk. 9And immediately the man was made whole, and took up his bed, and walked: and on the same day was the Sabbath (John 5:1-9).

This miracle of healing centers on a man who had been sick for a very long time. But first I want you to notice verse 3. 3In these lay a great multitude of impotent folk, of blind, halt, withered, waiting for the moving of the water (John 5:3). This was a place where many sick people gathered hoping to receive healing. Healthy people did not go near there. It must have been a sad sight: all kinds of sickness and disease. Can you hear the people crying and wailing?

The pool of Bethesda was like a mineral water bath that people believed healed them. Now in some translations, verse 4 is not included. According to tradition, an angel would stir up the waters. The first person to get into the water when it began to stir would be healed of their sickness or disability. Actually, the water only appeared to be "stirred." The cause was really that it was fed by underground springs that would periodically surge and cause the water to move. Let me make something very clear. Angels do not heal people. Are you listening to me? They do not have the ability to heal. I do not believe that an angel ever healed anyone. I believe that the power of God, working through people, is what helps our healing manifest.

Look at verse 5. This man had been sick for thirty-eight years. Can you imagine that? One year turned into two years, then into five years, then into ten years, then into twenty years. And then, he had been lying there for thirty-eight years. Some of you give up on God after your head has been hurting for one hour! But one day, everything changed. Here's verse 6. When Jesus saw him lie, and knew that he had been now a long time in that case, he saith unto him, Wilt thou be made whole?

Jesus knew that the man had been sick. To ask him if he wanted to be made whole must have seemed like a silly question. I believe Jesus was trying to see whether the man had the faith to be healed.

After being sick for so long, the man could have just made up his mind that he was going to lay there until he died. Are you at that point in your life? Have you said "well I've been sick this long, I guess I'll just be like this until I die? I came along to tell you don't think like that. All it takes is one instant and you can be healed. So I believe that Jesus was not just asking the man if he wanted to be made whole. He was asking the man "Do you believe that you can be made whole?"

The man's response is interesting. Jesus just asked him if he wanted to be made completely whole and he started making excuses. Verse 7: 7The impotent man answered him, Sir, I have no man, when the water is troubled, to put me into the pool: but while I am coming, another steppeth down before me. He was explaining why he thought he wasn't healed. Make sure you don't make excuses for your sickness and disease. I told you before – there is a simple explanation: the enemy brings sickness and disease, but Jesus has come to make us whole. Jesus didn't even address the man's excuses. As a matter of fact, we could just take verse 7 out. It doesn't matter how long you've been sick or why you are sick. Jesus comes to make you whole.

Jesus gave the man three simple commands: (Verse 8) Jesus saith unto him, Rise, take up thy bed, and walk. And then in verse 9: And immediately the man was made whole, and took up his bed, and walked. It said that immediately the man was made whole. I'm telling you it happened just like that. What I want you to see is that the man was made whole. There is a big difference between being healed and being made whole. Healing only addresses one aspect of our being. Wholeness speaks to your spirit, soul and body. So this man was not only healed in his physical body, I believe he was made totally whole. Every area of his life was made new in that moment. By following the commands of Jesus, you, too can be made totally whole.

When the people saw that the man had been made whole, they did not rejoice with him. I know that they knew how long this man had been sick. They must have known how long he had been lying there waiting to be healed. They didn't start praising God for healing their brother. No, they got upset because the man was healed on the Sabbath day! 10The Jews therefore said unto him that was cured, It is the Sabbath day: it is not lawful for thee to carry thy bed. They weren't concerned that the man was healed. In their religious eyes, it was wrong for him to be healed on that day. I'm sure the man didn't care that it was the Sabbath. All he knew was that after all those long years he was made whole.

Now when you receive your healing, there are going to be people who aren't going to be happy for you. They might be upset because you went to a healing crusade and received your healing instead of at their dead, dry church. They might be upset because you had on pants instead of a skirt when the power of God touched your life. Who cares about when it happens or where it happens. All I want you to do is be healed. And that's all Jesus wants, too. 16And therefore did the Jews persecute Jesus, and sought to slay him, because he had done these things on the Sabbath day. 17But Jesus answered them, My Father worketh hitherto, and I work. 18Therefore the Jews sought the more to kill him, because he not only had broken the sabbath, but said also that God was his Father, making himself equal with God.

The more Jesus talked, the angrier these people got. They wanted to kill him. But look at what Jesus said: 19Then answered Jesus and said unto them, Verily, verily, I say unto you, The Son can do nothing of himself, but what he seeth the Father do: for what things soever he doeth, these also doeth the Son likewise. 20For the Father loveth the Son, and sheweth him all things that himself doeth: and he will shew him greater works than these, that ye may marvel. Jesus told them "I'm only doing what I've seen my Father do." This is a good point to address some of the healing gimmicks I have seen and heard of. Jesus told them that He was only doing what he saw Father God do. That lets me know that if we don't see in scripture where God or Jesus did a certain thing, then we can't expect to do those things and receive our healing. I don't believe in selling miracle water and anointed oil. At my church we don't sell prayer cloths and gold dust. I just do not believe that any of these things get people healed. I'm telling you keep your money. All you need to do is believe that God is a healer and put yourself in a position to receive your healing.

An Eye Made of Mud

This account in John chapter 9 relates to a blind man who received his healing. The first thing I want you to notice is that it is the disciples who raise the question as to why the man is blind. 1And as Jesus passed by, he saw a man which was blind from his birth.2 And his disciples asked him, saying, Master, who did sin, this man, or his parents, that he was born blind? (John 9:1-2)

Now the disciples were with Jesus all the time. They knew Jesus was able to heal this man. They had seen Him heal many others before. But they still did not really know who Jesus was. If they had, they would not have asked this question. What does it really matter how the man got blind? The fact is that he was blind and Jesus was able to make him see again.

Don't fall into the trap of trying to understand why you are sick. Don't believe people when they say things like "Brother, God is just trying to get your attention." Or, " Sister you're just paying for all those years you lived in sin."" These are lies, lies, lies. I've told you before, but I'll say it again - it is the enemy who brings sickness and disease. It is that simple.

Here's what Jesus said in response to the disciples' question: 3Jesus answered, Neither hath this man sinned, nor his parents: but that the works of God should be made manifest in him. Now let me make this clear – Jesus was not saying that God gave the man blindness. He was simply saying that this was another situation in which the power of God could be displayed.

Here's another interesting thought in verse 4 and 5: I must work the works of him that sent me, while it is day: the night cometh, when no man can work.5As long as I am in the world, I am the light of the world. Jesus was saying that there was still time to work. And folks, let me tell you, we still have time for healing. You still have time to be healed and you still have time to teach others the truth about healing. Are you alive? Well then it's not too late. If you can understand the things that I am teaching, then you can receive your healing. More than that, you can keep your healing!

Jesus redeemed us from all sickness and disease. Here's another reason why Jesus told the disciples that it wasn't the mother or father's fault that the man was blind. We have been delivered from the iniquities of our forefathers. There is a difference between sin and iniquity. Iniquities may be passed down from generation to generation. If your father was a drunk and you don't deal with it and take authority over it, then you can become an alcoholic and then you can pass it down to your children. Sickness and disease can also be passed down. "Well, mama had diabetes and daddy had it too, I guess I'll get it next." The devil is a liar. You have the power to take authority over every sickness and every disease.

Look at John 9 verse 6: When he had thus spoken, he spat on the ground, and made clay of the spittle, and he anointed the eyes of the blind man with the clay. Even this blind man knew enough not to question the method that Jesus used. But don't you just wonder what the man was thinking when all this happened? I mean Jesus took spit and mud and I believe he literally made an eyeball out of the mud. I bet that man was thinking, "Well nothing else has worked, I might as well try this."

In verse 7, Jesus said "Go, wash in the pool of Siloam, (which is by interpretation, Sent.) He went his way therefore, and washed, and came seeing. Now I want you to notice that Jesus gave this man specific directions and the man followed the directions and got God results. He went away blind, but when he came back he could see. The man had to do something. You have to do something if you want to receive your healing. It will do you no good to sit there day after day and feel sorry for yourself. I challenge you to learn what the Word of God has to say about healing and then do something. Get up from there! You've got work to do.

After the man received his healing, all his "neighbors" came to see what had happened. They asked him, (verse 10) "How were your eyes opened"? So the man said(11) A man that is called Jesus made clay, and anointed mine eyes, and said unto me, Go to the pool of Siloam, and wash: and I went and washed, and I received sight. To the man it was that simple. He said, " I went, I washed, I received." But the people, especially the religious ones, kept asking him questions. "Who did it?" "How did he do it?" "Why did He do it today (on a Sabbath)?" The man just kept on saying the same thing. " Jesus anointed me, and told me to go and wash. I went, I washed, I received." When the man wouldn't say anything bad about Jesus or about the fact that Jesus had healed on the Sabbath, the people went to the man's parents. (Verses 18 - 22) 18But the Jews did not believe concerning him, that he had been blind, and received his sight, until they called the parents of him that had received his sight. 19And they asked them, saying, Is this your son, who ye say was born blind? how then doth he now see? 20His parents answered them and said, We know that this is our son, and that he was born blind: 21But by what means he now seeth, we know not; or who hath opened his eyes, we know not: he is of age; ask him: he shall speak for himself.22These words spake his parents, because they feared the Jews: for the Jews had agreed already, that if any man did confess that he was Christ, he should be put out of the synagogue.

The man's parents might have known the truth. Who else but the man's parents would have known what an awesome miracle this was. But they did not want to say what they knew was the truth. You know why? They were scared of the religious people. They were afraid they would get put out of their church. I'm telling you - you have to be determined to get your healing. When the religious people start telling you things like "We don't believe in healing. We don't believe in laying on hands and anointing with oil" then you have to make a decision. Is it more important for you to get healed or do you just want to stay there in religion and die?

The religious people were trying to trap Jesus. They wanted someone to say, for sure, that it was Jesus who did the healing and that it was Jesus who healed on a Sabbath. When the man's parents wouldn't say what the religious people wanted them to say, the people went back to the man and asked him again. "Who healed you and how did it happen?" The man basically told them "Say whatever you want to say, all I know is I was blind but now I can see" (verse 25)

The people tried to convince the man that Jesus was not sent from God and that the works Jesus was doing were not of God. But the man knew the truth. He said, "(verse 31) If this man were not of God, he could do nothing. Since the people knew that they were not going to be able to get to Jesus, they settled for throwing the man out of their "church." To tell the truth, he was much better off without all those religious voices shouting. Just like that man, you are going to have to make a decision. Do you believe Jesus has already paid the price for your healing? When you receive your healing are you going to be strong enough to stand up against religion? You have got to be able to stand by your beliefs even if it causes you to be put out of your "church."

Pigs and Demons

1And they came over unto the other side of the sea, into the country of the Gadarenes. 2And when he was come out of the ship, immediately there met him out of the tombs a man with an unclean spirit, 3Who had his dwelling among the tombs; and no man could bind him, no, not with chains: 4Because that he had been often bound with fetters and chains, and the chains had been plucked asunder by him, and the fetters broken in pieces: neither could any man tame him. 5And always, night and day, he was in the mountains, and in the tombs, crying, and cutting himself with stones. 6But when he saw Jesus afar off, he ran and worshipped him, 7And cried with a loud voice, and said, What have I to do with thee, Jesus, thou Son of the most high God? I adjure thee by God, that thou torment me not. 8For he said unto him, Come out of the man, thou unclean spirit. 9And he asked him, What is thy name? And he answered, saying, my name is Legion: for we are many. 10And he besought him much that he would not send them away out of the country. 11Now there was there nigh unto the mountains a great herd of swine feeding. 12And all the devils besought him, saying, Send us into the swine, that we may enter into them. 13And forthwith Jesus gave them leave. And the unclean spirits went out, and entered into the swine: and the herd ran violently down a steep place into the sea, (they were about two thousand;) and were choked in the sea. 14And they that fed the swine fled, and told it in the city, and in the country. And they went out to see what it was that was done. 15And they come to Jesus, and see him that was possessed with the devil, and had the legion, sitting, and clothed, and in his right mind: and they were afraid. 16And they that saw it told them how it befell to him that was possessed with the devil, and also concerning the swine. 17And they began to pray him to depart out of their coasts. 18And when he was come into the ship, he that had been possessed with the devil prayed him that he might be with him. 19Howbeit Jesus suffered him not, but saith unto him, Go home to thy friends, and tell them how great things the Lord hath done for thee, and hath had compassion on thee. (Mark 5:1-19)

The first point I want to make here is that this account is in direct contrast to Mark Chapter 4, where a great storm had arisen and the disciples had run to Jesus. They were almost paralyzed with the fear that the boat was going to sink. The storm had been a big one and the disciples thought that Jesus had abandoned them. The Lord rebuked the disciples for their lack of faith in Him and all that He had taught them.

When it comes to receiving and keeping your healing,

you have to just make up your mind. Jesus told the disciples – "We are going to the other side." And that's just what you have to say. It doesn't matter how long you have been suffering with whatever sickness and disease. Make up your mind – I am healed and I am going to walk in my healing. After the disciples were convinced that Jesus was trustworthy, no devil in hell could stop them from going to the other side. And so it is with your healing. When you finally make up your mind, there is no force of evil that is strong enough to keep you from being healed and staying healed.

Jesus spoke to the storm and immediately there was calm. When you find yourself in a "storm" and all kinds of aches and pains arise, just remind yourself that you are already healed. Then you can walk in peace, knowing that your body has no choice but to line up with the word of God.

So in this account, Jesus and the disciples had gone to the other side. They had faced and conquered the storm. The other side was a city called Gadarenes. "Then they sailed to the country of the Gadarenes, which is opposite Galilee. (verse 27) And when He stepped out on the land, there met Him a certain man from the city who had demons for a long time." Maybe you are like this man. Maybe you have been sick for a long time. I came to tell you that it doesn't matter how long you have been sick or what the sickness is. God is willing and able to heal you.

Let me stop for a moment and talk about demon possession. The scriptures say that this man had had demons for a long time. Now there is a difference between demon possession and demonic oppression. Now I am not one to believe that every bad thing that happens to a person is because they are possessed by demons. As a matter of fact, I don't believe that a Christian can be possessed by demons. Let me tell you why. The bible declares that darkness and light cannot abide in the same place. Once you receive Christ, the light of God replaces all the power of darkness in your life. A Christian cannot be possessed by a demon since he is filled with the Holy Spirit.

Demons are real, but we don't have to be afraid of them. As a matter of fact, we have power over them. I wish I had known this truth when I first started in the ministry. I remember one night we were having prayer and they brought in this lady who was possessed by demons. I thought I was this big, bad Christian and I began to talk to those demons. Now notice I said I talked to the demons. Folks, that is not smart. I'm telling you this went on and on for hours. I asked, "What is your name?" In a deep masculine voice, they growled, "We are legion. There are many of us." Every time I would try to talk to the lady, she would pass out. I finally got tired and I told the people who had brought the lady "Y'all take her on home – I'm done." Now today, I know better. I don't talk to demons anymore. I just take authority over them and command them to go.

Demonic oppression is altogether different. I do believe that a person can be a Christian and be the target of demonic oppression. As a matter of fact, that is the enemy's goal. He wants to keep you so beat down and depressed and oppressed that you never rise up and understand who you really are in Christ. As a believer, if you ever really find out who you are and what authority you have, you will never again be oppressed by demonic powers. They have no right to operate in your life and when you take authority over them, they have to go in the name of Jesus.

So the man in Gadarenes lived in a cemetery. He was so bound by the powers of darkness. He shrieked and wailed all night long, as he cut his body with stones. And he was strong, too. He would break out of the chains and shackles that people put on him. The people had tried to help him, but he was so far gone that even the ones who had cared for him had now left him alone to wander in the cemetery.

Maybe your situation is similar to this man. Have you been sick for so long that even the people who "love" you now just leave you alone and let you suffer in your sickness? "Well mama's been diagnosed with terminal cancer. All we can try to do is make her comfortable until she goes to be with the Lord." No! I'm telling you – you do not have to suffer with sickness and disease. It is God's will to heal you right now!

This man was alone and wandering in the cemetery. I'm sure the people thought there was no hope for him. But the man had enough sense to recognize Jesus and what Jesus was able to do for him. Even the demons recognized the power of the living God. "When he saw Jesus, he cried out, fell down before Him, and with a loud voice said, "What have I to do with You, Jesus, Son of the Most High God? I beg You, do not torment me! (verse 7)" Now this was not the man himself talking. This was the demons speaking through the man. Unlike the religious rulers of the day the demons immediately recognized that Jesus was indeed the Son of God. It is reassuring to note that Satan and his demons do not stand a chance when they come into contact with the full force of God's power.

Look at verse 8. The only thing that Jesus had to do was speak to the demons and immediately they obeyed. Let me tell you this – as far as God is concerned, when we speak healing, it is already accomplished. As far as God is concerned, you already had your healing when Jesus died on the cross. Jesus simply spoke to the demons and commanded them to come out. I'm telling you there is power in your words. When you speak healing, it is already done in the spirit. Now you just have to see it manifest in your physical body.

In verse 12, the demons asked for permission to go into the herd of swine. There might have been several reasons for this, but I want you to note that demons have no power unless they have a body to operate through. Now they don't care whether it's a human's body or a pig's body. They just have to have a body to operate through. The demonic spirits knew two things. One, they had to leave the man's body because Jesus had commanded them to go. Two, in order to continue their assignment of torment, they had go into some other body. So that's why they asked to go into the swine.

Now I'm not saying people aren't smarter than pigs. But look at verse 13. Even the pigs were smart enough to know that it is a miserable life being tormented by demonic spirits every day. The shock of suddenly being occupied by the demon spirits caused the pigs to blindly charge down the hillside into the lake to rid themselves of their unwanted guests. These pigs preferred suicide to demon possession. When are you going to rise up and realize that you do not have to put up with the oppression of sickness and disease that the enemy tries to bring? Get up from there. You are already healed and it's time to walk in it.

Jesus Stops The Bleeding

21And when Jesus was passed over again by ship unto the other side, much people gathered unto him: and he was nigh unto the sea.22And, behold, there cometh one of the rulers of the synagogue, Jairus by name; and when he saw him, he fell at his feet,23And besought him greatly, saying, My little daughter lieth at the point of death: I pray thee, come and lay thy hands on her, that she may be healed; and she shall live.24And Jesus went with him; and much people followed him, and thronged him.25And a certain woman, which had an issue of blood twelve years,26And had suffered many things of many physicians, and had spent all that she had, and was nothing bettered, but rather grew worse,27When she had heard of Jesus, came in the press behind, and touched his garment.28For she said, If I may touch but his clothes, I shall be whole.29And straightway the fountain of her blood was dried up; and she felt in her body that she was healed of that plague.30And Jesus, immediately knowing in himself that virtue had gone out of him, turned him about in the press, and said,

Who touched my clothes? 31 And his disciples said unto him, Thou seest the multitude thronging thee, and sayest thou, Who touched me? 32 And he looked round about to see her that had done this thing. 33 But the woman fearing and trembling, knowing what was done in her, came and fell down (Mark 5:21-32)

The first thing I want you see about the woman who had the issue of blood is that she already had her thinking straight. Like I've said before, you have got to have your mind made up when it comes to receiving and keeping your healing. Look at verse 25. This woman had had the same problem for twelve long years. It would have been easy for her to give up. She might have said, "Well, it's been this long and nothing has worked. I guess I'll just be like this until I die." But no, she was determined to get her healing. Are you determined today? Verse 26 tells us that she had gone to doctor after doctor and no one was able to help her. Instead of getting better, she got worse. Now all her money was gone and she still had the same problem. All the doctors had helped her do was stay broke miserable and disgusted.

Now I like verse 27. She heard about Jesus. What did she hear? She heard how he went about doing good, healing all those that were oppressed of the enemy. When we hear about God and Jesus, it produces faith. "So then faith cometh by hearing, and hearing by the word of God." (Romans 10:17). It's not enough to hear the word of God. True faith takes action. Lets read on. In verse 28, she shows that she had the faith for healing. She didn't say, "I might be healed." She said, " I shall be made well." I want you to notice her faith had gotten so strong that nobody could talk her out of what she believed. She had absolutely no doubt. She knew that Jesus was a healer and she knew that he would heal her. Proverbs 18:21 (KJV) tells us that death and life are in the power of the tongue. This woman chose to speak life. You have to do the same thing if you want to get your healing.

In Luke's account of this miracle (Luke 8: 44-47), it says that the woman came up from behind and touched the hem of Jesus' garment. She probably did this because the religious people would not have allowed her to get close to Jesus if they knew she was in the crowd. She was unclean because she was bleeding. In the eyes of the religious people, she did not deserve to get close enough to get her healing. But she decided to risk it all so that she could be healed.

Sometimes you have to get like this woman. Now I'm not saying that you shouldn't go to the doctor. But if you do go to the doctor and you get a bad report, you immediately have a decision to make. Do you believe what the doctor says or do you believe what the Word of God says. In that instant, you seal yourself. Whatever you believe the most, that is what you will receive. So this woman's faith in operation produced her healing. Look at verse 29. It says immediately the fountain of her blood was dried up. Immediately. I'm telling you: you can have instant healing if you can just believe God.

The last thing I want to bring out about this woman's miracle is Jesus reaction to the woman's touch. After she touched him, Jesus said, "Who touched me?" Now you and I both know that Jesus knew who had touched him. Do you think that the Jesus Christ does not know everything, even the end from the beginning? Jesus knew it was this woman who had touched him, but he made her make the public confession.

Look at what he said. … and when he saw her, he said, Daughter, be of good comfort; thy faith hath made thee whole. And the woman was made whole from that hour (Matthew 9:22 KJV)

I want you to see that there is a difference between being healed and being made whole. Not only did Jesus deliver the woman from the sickness that she had endured for twelve years, he made her whole. She was one hundred percent whole in her body, spirit, and soul. You can walk in that same wholeness if you get a hold of what I'm trying to teach you here.

This woman operated in faith, not fear. I remember a time when my children were in a car wreck. The police called on the phone to notify us that there had been an accident. Now being a father, of course I had the opportunity to think the worst and all kinds of images tried to rise up in my mind. But I told my wife, "When we get to the wreck scene, you are not to react in fear. We are going to operate in faith, and if He has to, God is going to raise our children from the dead." When we got there, our children were okay. The ambulance took them to the hospital to be checked. I asked one of the officers what happened. He told me that our children had pulled out in front of another young girl's car and that the other girl was dead. Immediately, faith rose in me and I yelled out "In the name of Jesus, she'll live and not die." The officer just looked at me kind of funny and started backing up.

When we got to the hospital, I asked the attendants, what happened to the other young girl? One of the paramedics who had been in the ambulance that transported the young girl said, "Sir, it was the strangest thing. When we were at the scene she had no pulse. We put her in the ambulance and began working on her. She still had no pulse. After a few minutes, she coughed and started breathing again." I just thanked God at that moment. I did not react in fear, that's what made the difference. I reacted in faith, and the Glory of God was revealed.

Let me share another account of faith in action. One day I was at the tire shop that my family owns. I had been reading books and studying the great men of faith and asking God to use me in the healing ministry. All of a sudden, I heard something crash into the window of the building. I went to see what it was, and there laid a dead bird at my feet. I could tell that the bird had broken its neck when it crashed into the window. I bent down and picked the bird up and started towards the trashcan to throw the bird away.

On the way to the trash, I heard the voice of the Lord speak: "If you can't raise a bird from the dead, you'll never raise a human being from the dead." Immediately, I took the bird and sat it on top of a car. I was eyeball to eyeball to that little dead bird and I began to speak to it. "Bird I command you to come back to life and fly." Nothing happened and I just continued talking to that bird. All of a sudden a larger bird swooped down and knocked that bird off of the car and down at my feet. I responded "Oh, no devil! You have no power or authority here."

As the little bird lay at my feet, I continued to speak life to it. After a little while, the little bird's wings began to flutter. It hopped up to its feet and looked up at me as if to say, "I appreciate that – thank you very much." The bird fluttered its wings once more and flew off. I knew then that the same faith that can raise a bird from the dead could raise a human from the dead. I never forgot that little bird and since then God has used me in many miraculous ways.

A Dead Girl Lives

22 And, behold, there cometh one of the rulers of the synagogue, Jairus by name; and when he saw him, he fell at his feet, 23 And besought him greatly, saying, My little daughter lieth at the point of death: I pray thee, come and lay thy hands on her, that she may be healed; and she shall live. 24 And Jesus went with him; and much people followed him, and thronged him….35 While he yet spake, there came from the ruler of the synagogue's house certain which said, Thy daughter is dead: why troublest thou the Master any further? 36 As soon as Jesus heard the word that was spoken, he saith unto the ruler of the synagogue, Be not afraid, only believe. 37 And he suffered no man to follow him, save Peter, and James, and John the brother of James. 38 And he cometh to the house of the ruler of the synagogue, and seeth the tumult, and them that wept and wailed greatly. 39 And when he was come in, he saith unto them, Why make ye this ado, and weep? the damsel is not dead, but sleepeth. 40 And they laughed him to scorn. But when he had put them all out, he taketh the father and the

mother of the damsel, and them that were with him, and entereth in where the damsel was lying. 41 And he took the damsel by the hand, and said unto her, Talitha cumi; which is, being interpreted, Damsel, I say unto thee, arise. 42 And straightway the damsel arose, and walked; for she was of the age of twelve years. And they were astonished with a great astonishment. 43 And he charged them straitly that no man should know it; and commanded that something should be given her to eat. (Mark 5:22-24,35-42 KJV)

This miracle actually parallels with the miracle of the woman who was healed of the issue of blood. As a matter of fact, it was Jairus who came to Jesus first to tell him about his sick daughter. After Jairus had told Jesus what the problem was, the woman with the issue of blood approached Jesus and got her miracle.

So I want you to look at this. Jairus came to Jesus and said, "My daughter is sick. She is about to die. Please come and lay your hands on her and she will live." See how he spoke in faith? Now Jairus knew that this was a serious situation. But look at what he said - she shall live. I'm telling you your confession brings possession. I remember when we first started our church, we all used to have confession sheets. We would hang them on the mirrors, on the refrigerators. We would tape them everywhere. Do you know what that did? It kept the Word of God before us. Everywhere you turned there was a scripture. It built our faith. Now we've gotten away from that. I guess we're too busy or that we think we don't need to do those confessions anymore. But I'm telling you – what you say out of your own mouth will come to pass. I don't care if you are sick as a buzzard. If you confess with your mouth and act in faith, you can be healed.

So Jairus said, " Jesus, my daughter is dying but if you touch her I know she will live." Jesus immediately left to follow Jairus to his house. While they were on the way, one of the people from Jairus' house met them and said "Your daughter is dead, Jairus. Don't bother Jesus anymore." Immediately, Jesus spoke to Jairus and told him not to be afraid. This is powerful. If you can resist the urge to fear when sickness and disease comes, you can have the victory. Now I know it's easy to get scared when the doctor says you have cancer and you will be dead in two months. Don't get into fear. Fear and faith do not mix. You either have total faith or no faith. If you give any place to fear, then you open the door for the enemy to come in and steal, kill and destroy. Jesus told Jairus not to be afraid. Now I'm telling you, don't be afraid. It doesn't matter what it is – you can overcome it if you stay in faith.

Notice that Jesus sent everyone away except for Peter, James, and John. Sometimes you have to get everyone out of the way so that you can just believe God. If people are doubting and speaking contrary to the Word of God, get them out from around you. Jesus sent every one away so that he could operate in the Power of God. When they got to the house, all the professional mourners were doing their job. They were screaming and hollering and carrying on. Jesus said, " Why are y'all making such a fuss? The little girl is not dead, she's just sleeping." Remember the story of Lazarus. Jesus had said the same thing - "our friend Lazarus sleepeth" (John 11:11, KJV). Now Jesus knew that Lazarus was dead and he knew that this little girl was dead. The people laughed and laughed. They thought, "Well, poor old Jesus – He's finally lost it. This girl is deader than a doorknob and He thinks she's just asleep."

Jesus put everyone out except the little girl's mother and father, Jairus. I'm going to say it again. You have got to get away from people who don't believe like you do. If you believe that Jesus is a healer and that he is your healer, then you can't afford to be around people who talk doubt and unbelief. Once all of the doubters were gone, it was easy for Jesus to do the work. He just took the girl by the hand and told her to arise. The little girl got right up! When you operate in faith, it is that easy. Just get all the fear, doubt and unbelief out, and you can walk in your healing.

A Brand New Set of Legs

This is the only miracle that I will cover that was not performed by Jesus. But I want you to know that we have the same healing power as Jesus had. I know that might be a little hard for you to believe, but look at John 14:2 - Verily, verily, I say unto you, He that believeth on me, the works that I do shall he do also; and greater works than these shall he do; because I go unto my Father (KJV). Peter and John were doing the greater works.

1Now Peter and John went up together into the temple at the hour of prayer, being the ninth hour.2And a certain man lame from his mother's womb was carried, whom they laid daily at the gate of the temple which is called Beautiful, to ask alms of them that entered into the temple;3Who seeing Peter and John about to go into the temple asked an alms.4And Peter, fastening his eyes upon him with John, said, Look on us.5And he gave heed unto them, expecting to receive something of them.6Then Peter said, Silver and gold have I none; but such as I have give I thee: In the name of Jesus Christ of Nazareth rise up and walk.7And he took him by the right hand, and lifted him up: and immediately his feet and ankle bones received strength.8And he leaping up stood, and walked, and entered with them into the temple, walking, and leaping, and praising God. 9And all the people saw him walking and praising God: 10And they knew that it was he which sat for alms at the Beautiful gate of the temple: and they were filled with wonder and amazement at that which had happened unto him. 11And as the lame man which was healed held Peter and John, all the people ran together unto them in the porch that is called Solomon's, greatly wondering.12And when Peter saw it, he answered unto the people, Ye men of Israel, why marvel ye at this? Or why look ye so earnestly on us, as though by our own power or holiness we had made this man to walk? 13The God of Abraham, and of Isaac, and of Jacob, the God of our fathers, hath glorified his Son Jesus… 16And his name through faith in his name hath made this man strong, whom ye see and know: yea, the faith which is by him hath given him this perfect soundness in the presence of you all (Acts 3:1-14,16 KJV)

Let me start in verse 2. This man had never walked a day in his life. It says he was lame when he was born. It is a miracle in itself that his bones had developed. Doctors say if you don't use your muscles and exercise them, eventually you lose all ability to move. So, every day people would carry this man to the temple gate. Now this is a good place for me to tell you this: you do not have to depend on somebody else to believe for your healing. Stop letting your mama or your grandma or you preacher "carry" you. You can believe God for yourself. You can do it!

The disciples must have passed by this man everyday. Peter and John were men of God and I know they went to the temple every day at prayer time. So they knew this man and this man knew them. Peter and John must have given this man money many times before. Why else would the man have asked them for money on that day? Look at verse 5: And he gave heed unto them, expecting to receive something of them. You don't ask someone for something if you know they don't have it to give. It said Peter and John were not some broke, miserable and disgusted Christians who were just trying to hang on and endure. These men were fishermen before becoming disciples, so you know they were good businessmen.

Peter and John had money. These men were going to the house of God. You should never go to the house of God without taking a gift. Peter and John knew how to treat God. They must have had money to present as an offering. But isn't it amazing, Peter told the man "we don't have any money for you today." What Peter was really saying is this: " We could give you money, but today do you want something more than money? Do you want to receive your healing so that you don't have to beg anymore?" They were asking the man if he wanted to be different. Now I'm asking you the same thing. Do you want to receive your healing?

Peter and John did not give the man a chance to respond or give excuses. Peter simply said "We're not going to give you money today. We are going to give you something much better!" When you are dealing with people who need healing, don't give them time to object. If you know that they want to receive healing and the healing power of God is in operation, then just do like Peter and John did. They said, "In the name of JESUS, get up!" I'm telling you the name of Jesus is so great that all you have to do is speak the Name and you can receive your healing. 9Wherefore God also hath highly exalted him, and given him a name which is above every name: 10That at the name of Jesus every knee should bow, of things in heaven, and things in earth, and things under the earth (Philippians 2:9-10).

The man received his healing immediately. He didn't have to pray and say, "If it's your will God..." It is always God's will to heal. The man got up. His legs, ankles, and feet received strength, and for the first time in his whole life, the man began to walk. Here is another key to keeping your healing. Look how the man responded: And he leaping up stood, and walked, and entered with them into the temple, walking, and leaping, and praising God (verse 8). As soon as he received his healing, the man went to the house of God. He went to praise God. Now he could have gone anywhere. He could have said, "This is cause for celebration, I'm going down to the local bar and get me a cold one." No, he knew that it was the Power of God that had healed him and he went to God's house to give Him praise. When you receive your healing, remember Who it is that healed you.

The people were amazed that this man was healed. I'm sure some of the people who carried him around everyday could hardly believe their eyes. This was the last day that this man would need to be carried anywhere! The people began to look at Peter and John as if they were the healers. Peter and John knew the truth. They said, "let's get this straight – it was not us who healed this man. God has glorified Jesus and the Name of Jesus and faith in the Name of Jesus has healed this man."

Look at that again in verse 16 And his name through faith in his name hath made this man strong. There were two things in operation here: the Name of Jesus and faith in the name of Jesus. Here is the key, folks. To receive and keep your healing you have to first believe in the Name of Jesus. You have to believe that Jesus is who he said He is. Then, you have to believe, by faith, that the power that is in Jesus' name can heal you and keep you healed.

Abiding in the Vine

I want to teach you how to keep your healing. I have shared all these things with you, but it won't do you any good to get healed if you can't stay healed. So here is what I believe will keep you healed – you have got to stay in Him. Let's look at this:

1I am the true vine, and my Father is the husbandman .2Every branch in me that beareth not fruit he taketh away: and every branch that beareth fruit, he purgeth it, that it may bring forth more fruit.3Now ye are clean through the word which I have spoken unto you.4Abide in me, and I in you. As the branch cannot bear fruit of itself, except it abide in the vine; no more can ye, except ye abide in me. 5I am the vine, ye are the branches: He that abideth in me, and I in him, the same bringeth forth much fruit: for without me ye can do nothing. 6If a man abide not in me, he is cast forth as a branch, and is withered; and men gather them, and cast them into the fire, and they are burned. 7If ye abide in me, and my words abide in you, ye shall ask what ye will, and it shall be done unto you (John

15:1-7 KJV)

Now if you are saved, you already have the first part. Verse 4 says abide in me and I in you. If you have confessed Jesus, then He abides in you. Now you have to abide in Him. What does abide mean? It means to stay in or continue. So you have to stay in Jesus and continue in Him. Keep studying; keep meditating on the healing scriptures. Keep confessing that you were healed, you are healed, and you will stay healed.

You have to understand the natural meaning of what Jesus was saying here in order to understand what He really meant in the spirit. A vine is a climbing or spreading plant. In comparing himself to a vine, Jesus was saying that he wanted to be spread out. He has told us to spread the Gospel. He wants people to know the truth about healing. So when you receive your healing, share this book with someone else who needs healing. Let them see how it is the good will of the Father for us to get healed and to stay healed.

So Jesus is the vine and then it says that the Father is the husbandman. Now husbandman is just another word for a farmer. Any good farmer "purges" his plants. You have to get the weeds and the sticks out. You have to get out all that mess and stinking thinking that tells you that you are not worthy to be healed because of where you have been or what you have done.

Jesus is the vine and we are the branches that abide in the vine. We have to allow the Father, the farmer, to purge us. Once God, through His word, purges all the bad things out of you, and then you have to replace it with the truth. Replace it with the things that I'm teaching y'all, folks.

Look what it says happens after the purging. It says that the branches produce much more fruit. You can produce the fruit of healing. And you can keep on producing healing. How are you going to do it? You have got to stay in Jesus. Look at it again, then. I am the vine, ye are the branches: He that abideth in me, and I in him, the same bringeth forth much fruit: for without me ye can do nothing (verse 5). Get in the Word (Jesus) and stay in the Word, and you will produce fruit. It is emphatic. I'm telling you if you get a hold of the truth I have taught you, then there is no devil in hell that can keep you from getting your healing and keeping your healing.

In verse 6 it tells us what happens to the branch that does not produce fruit. Simply put, it is destroyed. That goes right along with the scripture that says "my people are destroyed for lack of knowledge (Hosea 4:6 KJV). Do not let yourself be destroyed when it comes to your healing. If you just apply the things that I'm teaching you, you will never be destroyed because you will know the truth.

Right here, let me say again that it is important that you continue in the things of God once you receive your healing. I remember a man by the name of Roger who attended my church years ago. When he and his family came to the church, they were not Christians. They started attending our church and we prayed the prayer of salvation with them. We received a call that the family needed us to pray for Roger. He was in the hospital with two tumors. Each tumor was about the size of a grapefruit. When I saw him at the hospital, the man did not even look like he weighed a hundred pounds. I spent the whole day, about six or eight hours with Roger. We prayed, commanding the tumors to dry up and die.

I left the hospital that night believing that our prayers were effective and that Roger was going to get better. The doctors did not even expect Roger to live through the night. But he did. The doctors were so amazed! The next day, they did all the x-rays to see what happened. The tumors were completely gone! Roger had been healed by the power of God! He had to stay in the hospital for about ten days so that the doctors could wean him off of the powerful pain medicine that he was on.

Roger came back to church after he was healed. He stayed for about two months and then his family left the church. I didn't see or hear from Roger for over ten years. As a matter of fact, I had heard that he died. But, one day, a man knocked on the door at the church. I answered the door and the man said, "You don't know who I am, do you?" I had to admit that I didn't know who the man was. He said, "It's me – Roger." I was so surprised to see him. He looked so good. He came in my office and we talked for a while. "How are you doing, Roger?" I asked. I will never forget what he said: "God gave me a second chance, and I'm partying to the max." It broke my heart that a man could be so gloriously healed and then not even serve the Healer.

I pray that you understand now that you can be healed. It is God's will for you to be healed. Now you have a decision to make. You have read the truth. Will you embrace it and see the healing power of God manifested in your life?

Healing is for Today

This chapter is designed to build your faith so that you can receive your healing. These are the testimonies of real people in my church who have seen the miraculous healing power of God. Listen to their stories and be blessed.

Jilayla Jackson

My name is Lisa Jackson and I am sharing the testimony of my daughter Jilayla. She was born on October 7, 2005. I was at 23 weeks gestation and I went into labor. My doctors tried to stop my contractions, but none of the medicine or techniques that they used worked. Finally, they decided that I would have to have an emergency Caesarian section to deliver my baby.

Jilayla weighed 1 pound and 6 ounces when she was born. You can't even imagine how tiny she was. Her lungs were not developed and she had several life threatening conditions. She was not breathing on her own. She had a brain bleed and low blood pressure. She was on full life support and the doctors told me that she had less than a thirty percent chance of survival. If she did survive, they told me, she would very likely have cerebral palsy or muscular dystrophy, or some other type of physical handicap. I decided that as long as there was any chance of survival, I would do all I could to save my baby.

When Jilayla was ten days old, I received a call from the hospital. The doctors told me that Jilayla had developed pulmonary interstitial emphysema (P I E). Basically, this meant that she had a hole in one of her, already under developed, lungs. She was too small for them to insert a chest tube or do any kind of surgery. I was told that she would probably only live a couple of more days.

I was hysterical. I had only been a member of the church since May of 2005, but I called Pastor Dean and asked him to come and pray for my baby because they were not expecting her to live very much longer. Pastor Dean told me to call back later that evening. When my husband got off work that evening, we called Pastor Dean and went to the church to pick him up. Together, we all went to the hospital to see Jilayla.

When we got to the hospital, Pastor Dean, Jilayla's father, Scott, and I went to Jilayla's bedside. Pastor Dean asked Scott about his spiritual life. Scott admitted that he was saved, but needed to rededicate his life to the Lord. Pastor Dean prayed with him. Then, Pastor Dean asked Scott and me what we wanted to happen. We both said we wanted our baby to live. Pastor Dean prayed over Jilayla and spoke life into her. With all three of us touching and agreeing, we began to thank God for a miracle.

Later that evening, I went back to Jilayla's bedside. One

of the doctors came by to check on her. He was checking her vital signs and using his stethoscope. I heard him say, "Oh, this is good." I knew at that moment that God had performed a miracle for my baby. They had given her a death sentence, but we spoke life and saw the glory of God revealed.

From that moment on, Jilayla did nothing but progress. From time to time she had little set backs, but all in all she did great. The hole in her lung closed up and she began to thrive. She was three weeks old before we could touch her and hold her. She was three months old before she could be fed from a bottle. In all, she stayed in the hospital for 134 days.

Every single day, I would go to the hospital and visit her. I would sit for hours and hours, just holding her and thanking God for healing her. Along the way, Jilayla has had a few hurdles to face. She had pneumonia and had to have several blood transfusions. , Over all, though, she is a normal healthy child. Of all the things that they said she would have: cerebral palsy, muscular dystrophy, mental retardation, she has none of them. Today, Jilayla is almost four years old (in 2009). She is active, healthy, and healed. All the glory belongs to God.

To the person seeking healing, I would say trust the Word of God. He has already said that healing is ours. Once you have received your healing, it is so important to continue to confess the Word of God. Every single day that Jilayla was in the hospital, I would speak the Word of God over her. I would quote scriptures. I still do this, even today, because I believe it is my job, as her mother, to make sure that Jilayla keeps her healing.

Also, it is important who you listen to. When Jilayla

was sick, I made it known that I did not want anyone around who was speaking doubt and unbelief. I even had to isolate myself and my baby from some of my family members. Anyone who said anything negative could not be around us.

I speak from my own personal experience when I say that God is a healer and healing is still for today. Just look at my daughter, Jilayla Jackson, and you will see for yourself.

Eddie Adams

My name is Debra Adams. I want to share my testimony regarding my son Eddie. One night, my younger son Jamar came and knocked on my bedroom door. When he came in, he was just staring at me. I asked him what was wrong and he said, "Mom, Eddie just got shot." Jamar didn't say anything else; he just ran out of the house and left in his car.

I felt fear try to take over me. It was like a burning sensation. It started in my feet and was traveling up my legs and had reached my thighs. I called on the name of Jesus and immediately the burning stopped. I knew I had to stay calm. I called Pastor Dean Melton and I told him everything that I knew. My son had been shot, but I didn't know where he was shot or how he was doing. Pastor Dean immediately began to quote scriptures to me. I specifically remember him quoting Ezekiel 16:6. He told me that my son would live and not die. He said, "Your son's blood will not be polluted."

I knew that Eddie was saved and that he loves the Lord. I later found out that Eddie had been on his way to take some of his cousins home. The place where he was going was a very bad neighborhood. When Eddie was shot, he said the Lord spoke to him and told him to put his fingers in the wound and keep driving because if he stopped, the shooter would fire more bullets. Eddie drove towards the hospital, but became so weak that he couldn't drive anymore. He got out of the car and lay on the sidewalk, hoping that someone would come and help him. He said he remembered a very kind police officer kneeling beside him and telling him, "You're not going to die." I believe that police officer was an angel.

When I received the news that Eddie had been shot, I began to call on the name of Jesus. I called several people who I knew would be praying with me and not against me. I said "God I thank you for my son's life. I thank you that my son will not have brain damage. I thank you, Lord that all of my son's organs function properly. I thank you, Lord that my son will not be paralyzed." I was just praising God and thanking Him in advance for what he was about to do for my son and me.

Let me also say this. While I was at my house that night, I literally saw Jesus and His angels. I also saw satan and his demons. I couldn't see any faces, but I knew who everyone was. Jesus had something in his hand. After he dealt with satan, Jesus pointed at me and said, "Your child will live!" Tears of joy ran down my face and from that moment on, I had total peace about the situation.

I stayed at my house for about two or three hours. My family was calling me from the hospital. The kept asking "Where are you and when are you going to get here?" I knew that I had to spend time with my God, so I just stayed home until I felt like it was time to go to the hospital. When I got to the hospital, my family said, "Where have you been and what took you so long to get here?" I just kept walking. I was on a mission and I had to see Eddie.

When I saw Eddie, he said "Mom I begged them not to call you because I didn't want to worry you." He said, "Mom, I didn't die – I'm alive." I said, " I know baby, because my God told me that you were going to live." I spoke with the doctors and they said they had to rush Eddie to CT-scan to see how many bullet wounds he had and to see how extensive the wounds were. I told them to go ahead and do what they had to do. But I also told them that my son would not have to have surgery and that God had already told me that He was going to work on my behalf.

When the doctors came back with the CT-scan report, they told me that Eddie was lucky. I knew that he was not lucky because I don't believe in luck. I believe in the healing power of the almighty GOD. The doctor said it was actually one bullet that split in two when it entered Eddie's head. "The good news", the doctor said, "is that he will not have to have surgery. The bullet fragments will work themselves out." Praise, God! They moved Eddie from the emergency room to the 11th floor. By the time they got my son all cleaned up and ready for a private room, the doctors told us that he was actually ready to go home!

Today, Eddie is perfectly healthy. He has no problems that are related to the shooting incident. Just like the doctor said, the bullets worked themselves out. I just praise God for the teaching that I have received at Freedom Christian Center. I thank God that I knew the Word and when I was thrust into a very bad situation, I knew how to pray and I knew that my prayers would work.

Micah Flowe

The account of this healing is told from two perspectives. First, Deena McCorkle-Reid tells her account:

"Freedom Christian Center was having a Valentine's Day Party. My brother, Craig, and I were watching the nursery. We had about fifteen children. They were from age 3 months to 5 years. All of the rest of the children were very rowdy, but Micah was kind of quiet and was very clingy. He was hanging on to my brother.

About an hour went by and Craig asked me "Does Micah look okay to you?" I said "Maybe he's just sleepy." But as I stood there for a minute, I noticed that Micah's breathing was not normal and he was pale. His lips also looked different, but I didn't think anything was really wrong with him.

I went back to check on the infants. Not even five minutes went by and my brother called for me. When I looked at Micah, I knew something was wrong. His eyes were rolling back in his head and his lips were bluish in color. I screamed "Craig, pray right now!" My brother and I began to pray. Pastor Dean had been teaching us about the power of prayer and how we have the authority to minister one to another. We prayed in tongues and spoke life into Micah. We called on the name of Jesus and commanded healing virtue to flow.

Craig was holding Micah and Micah went limp. He didn't seem to be breathing. We kept praying and laid hands on him. Craig continued to hold Micah and I called over to the church to tell Micah's parents about the situation. Micah's mother arrived. From, there she can tell the rest of what happened.

Micah's mother Cathy Flowe tells the rest:
"We were at a church function one Saturday night. They called from the nursery and told me that something was wrong with my son, Micah. At the time, Micah was about two years old. I remember when I walked into the nursery; one of our teenagers, Craig McCorkle was holding Micah. Craig's sister Deena was walking the floor and praying in the Spirit. I looked at my baby and immediately, the mother in me switched off and the Holy Ghost took over. I just remember that he was stiff and his mouth was clenched tightly. I could tell he was having a convulsion.

I am trained in the medical field, so I knew I had to do something to keep him from swallowing his tongue. His hands were blue and his face was turning blue around the mouth. He was not breathing. I remember yelling, "Micah, in the Name of Jesus, I command you to live and not die." I screamed, "Devil, you take your hands off my baby."

I took Micah from Craig and started to walk back across the street. I had been listening to tapes and building myself up. In my physical body, I was tired and aggravated. But my spirit man was wide-awake. One of the tapes I had been listening to was regarding the widow of Zarephath. I remembered how the man of God had taken the dead baby from the woman and how, after Elijah prayed, the baby came back to life. I thought "I have got to get my baby to the man of God." I walked into the church and called for Pastor Dean.

Pastor Dean lay across my baby and began to command life to come back into his body. Everyone else in the church was praying and believing God for a miracle. Although I didn't think to, someone had called 911. I remember just before the paramedics got there, Micah took this long, deep breath. He began to return back to normal. By the time the paramedics started working on him, we knew that he was already healed.

We did go on to the hospital. They ran all kinds of tests. We stayed there all night long. They found nothing wrong with Micah. I knew it had been a trick of the enemy. Since we were still in Charlotte, we left the hospital and went straight back to church. When we walked in the door, the whole place exploded! We were all so happy that God had healed my baby.

Today, in 2009, Micah is almost 23 years old. He is a strong, active, young man. I thank God every day for him. I will never forget the night the enemy tried to take him from us. But, because the teenagers who were watching him knew their authority and because we all responded in the correct way – in faith, not in fear - we were able to see the healing power of God manifested.

Above All: Be In Health (3 John 1:2)

Wanda Melton Jolley

My name is Wanda Melton Jolley and I am blessed to have my father as my Pastor. Growing up, my dad didn't do things the way other dads did. I can't tell you how many times my brother and I have looked at each other and said "Dad is crazy."

But, there is something to be said about my dad being so different. He has instilled many truths into my brother and me. For example, when we were in school and we woke up not feeling well my dad would say, "You can't stay home if you are sick, but when you feel good, you can have a well day." That didn't make any sense to us, but we would get up, crying and fussing, and go on to school. Usually, by the time we got back home, we were healed. Those "well" days were definitely better than laying in the bed sick all day.

I can tell you many things about how my dad has taught me the truths of God. One time, when I was about ten years old, I was running through the woods and I ran right into a hornet's nest. I got stung about thirty times, so my mom decided that I needed to go to the hospital. At the hospital, the doctor gave me medicine and told my mom that I was severely allergic to bees. He told her that I would have to carry medicine around with me for the rest of my life because if I ever got stung again I would have to immediately take the medicine or I would die within minutes.

When we got home that day, my dad took the medicine and put it in the medicine cabinet. I remember him telling my mom and me that I would not be carrying that medicine around with me all the time because no daughter of his was going to be in bondage to some medicine. My mom, my brother and I didn't really understand that, but he was the dad and we were under his authority.

Years went by and then one day I was at the park with our children from summer day camp. A bee stung me. I didn't have the medicine with me. I didn't take the medicine, but I'm still alive and well today. Many parents would have made their children wear a medical bracelet, told all the teachers about the child's allergies, and maybe even wrote it on the child's forehead. My dad did not do any of those things. He knew the Word and he believed God.

Another time, my dad received a phone call. It was my uncle calling to tell us that my brother had been in an accident. My brother was at the water park going down the slide. The pressure of the water had pushed him off the side of the slide. He hit his head on a rock and swallowed a piece of the rubber mat that he was on. The piece of mat had become lodged in his windpipe. My uncle administered CPR and revived him. They took my brother to the hospital because they thought he had a ruptured spleen. My dad prayed and he never let my mother know what had happened.

The next day, my dad told my mom "Let's ride to the beach tomorrow to see our family." My mom still did not know what had happened to my brother. When we got to the beach, out came by brother, Ronnie. He was alive and well! Most people would have been in a panic, rushing to get to their child as quickly as they could. But, not my dad. He knew that God would take care of it and he waited until God told him to move.

When I was young, I didn't understand what my dad was doing or why he said what he did. Now that I am older, I realize that the dad I thought was so crazy was really just instilling trust and the faith of God in our lives. I have learned so many things from my dad. I now know that I do not have to live my life in fear.

Last year, in 2008, I was diagnosed with cancer. I had the opportunity to be defeated and cast down. But instead, because of my dad's teaching me all these years, I knew that Jesus was my healer. I knew that He would take care of me. Now, I am happy to say that I am free of cancer. I am healed!

My dad is an awesome man of God. He lives what he teaches. I am alive and well today because I have embraced the scriptures and teachings that you have just been reading about.

Your Time Is Now

I have given you numerous accounts of God's healing power at work. We have seen how God operated in biblical times and you have even read accounts of people who have been healed in our generation. Let me tell you: our God is the same yesterday, today and forever. We, as the children of the Most High God have every right and ability not only to walk in healing, but also to operate in healing. We have the same power, people. As a matter of fact, we are supposed to be operating on an even greater level. Look what Jesus said: Verily, verily, I say unto you, He that believeth on me, the works that I do shall he do also; and greater works than these shall he do; because I go unto my Father (John 14:12).

In the previous chapter, I included the accounts of people from my congregation. I want you to know that healing is not just for those with a title behind their name: pastor, apostle, Dr., etc. Folks, healing is for the believer. And these signs shall follow them that believe; In my name shall they cast out devils; they shall speak with new tongues; 18They shall take up serpents; and if they drink any deadly thing, it shall not hurt them; they shall lay hands on the sick, and they shall recover. (Mark 16:17-18)

Did you read what it said? It is emphatic. These signs shall follow you because you are a believer. You shall lay your hands on the sick and they shall recover. Understand that it is God who is the healer. When you do, it takes all of the pressure off you. It's not your responsibility to heal. It is your responsibility to believe and to lay your hands on the sick. Then, believe the word of God that says they shall be healed.

Don't believe the lie of the enemy. You are well able to overcome any sickness and disease. You already have the power of God. In Luke chapter 9, Jesus gave power to the disciples. Look at it: 1Then he called his twelve disciples together, and gave them power and authority over all devils, and to cure diseases. 2And he sent them to preach the kingdom of God, and to heal the sick (verse 1-2). Today, you and I are the Father's disciples. Put the power that God has given you into operation and receive your healing now!

So, believer, I challenge you. Read this book again and again until you can understand the truths that I have taught you here. I guarantee you that the Word of God is infallible. That is why I have based everything in this book on the Word.

Also, be sure to get in a church that teaches the word. You need to have a shepherd over your life – someone whom you can be accountable to. The man or woman of God is responsible to teach you the truth, but it is your job to walk in the truth after you have been taught. If you study the scriptures with an open heart, I know that you will agree: it is God's will that you be healed and that you stay healed. Above all, my friend, be in health and prosper.

To order additional copies of this book or Dr. Melton's other book, *The Love of Money*, please call 704-392-0137 or visit us on the web at www.fccministry.com. Dr. Melton also has various other teachings and ministry material available. We welcome your inquiries!

When you are in the Charlotte, NC area, we welcome you to visit Freedom Christian Center, where Dr. Melton serves as Pastor. We are a non-denominational, family friendly church.

Freedom Christian Center
4020 Freedom Drive
Charlotte, NC 28208